CHANGING Families

LGBT Families

Leanne Currie-McGhee

ReferencePoint Press®

San Diego, CA

ReferencePoint Press®

Printed in the United States

For more information, contact:
ReferencePoint Press, Inc.
PO Box 27779
San Diego, CA 92198
www.ReferencePointPress.com

LIBRARY OF CONGRESS CATALOGING-IN-PUBLICATION DATA

Name: Currie-McGhee, L.K. (Leanne K.) author.
Title: LGBT Families/by Leanne Currie-McGhee.
Description: San Diego, CA: ReferencePoint Press, [2019] | Series: Changing Families | Audience: Grade 9 to 12. | Includes bibliographical references and index.
Identifiers: LCCN 2018021280 (print) | LCCN 2018026185 (ebook) | ISBN 9781682823606 (eBook) | ISBN 9781682823590 (hardback)
Subjects: LCSH: Sexual minorities—Family relationships—Juvenile literature. | Sexual minority parents—Juvenile literature. | Children of sexual minority parents--Juvenile literature. | Gay parents—Juvenile literature. | Children of gay parents—Juvenile literature. | Families—Juvenile literature.
Classification: LCC HQ73 (ebook) | LCC HQ73 .C87 2019 (print) | DDC 306.76—dc23
LC record available at https://lccn.loc.gov/2018021280

Contents

Chapter One

How American Families Are Changing

Hope Steinman-Iacullo considers herself a strong, independent woman, and she attributes that to the way her parents raised her. They raised her with love, were active in her life, and always supported her. In all of these ways, Steinman-Iacullo's parents are like many other parents, but they differ in one significant way: they are both men.

Wayne Steinman and Sal Iacullo adopted Hope when she was a baby. "We became dads when our daughter, Hope, was placed in our arms in August 19, 1987 in New York City and she was four months old at the time," Steinman explains. "Sal was actually the lead parent in the adoption—he was the first openly gay male to experience single-parent adoption. However, we were both Hope's dads. We had legal papers, the court made sure from the get-go that we had both guardianship papers and wills so that if anything happened to Sal, Hope would become my child."[1]

Same-sex marriage was not legal at the time, and adoptions by same-sex couples were extremely rare, but Steinman and Iacullo had been together for years and were determined to have a family. They began the adoption process, but it was challenging because many agencies did not consider an openly gay person to be an appropriate parent. However, they persevered because they knew they could provide love and a stable upbringing to a child.

To them, it was love at first sight when Hope arrived, and they jumped into parenthood. For the most part, they lived a normal family life; yet at times they encountered prejudice and challenges. One such incident occurred during a road trip to Disney

World. At one point during their drive from New York to Florida, they stopped for lunch. While there, a police officer came up and questioned them. Because it was unusual to see a baby with two men, the officer felt he needed to make sure they had not kidnapped Hope. After much talking, they were able to convince the officer that they were her fathers. From that point on, they always carried their adoption papers with them.

Hope's Experience

Growing up, Steinman-Iacullo was aware, early on, that her family structure was not the same as most of her friends' families, but other than that, she felt that her life was similar to the lives of her friends. Her parents were very involved in her activities. At different times, both of her dads had served as president of the parent-teacher associations at her schools. They took her to her activities, helped her with homework, traveled on family vacations, and enjoyed all the aspects of a normal family.

> **"I think that my parents did a fantastic job of helping to raise me to be a strong woman."[2]**
>
> —Hope Steinman-Iacullo, the daughter of two dads

Sometimes, Steinman-Iacullo thought about how her life was different than others. "I knew that people had something called a mother that I didn't necessarily have, but I didn't really think that I was so much in the minority," she says. "I wondered about my birth family and my birth mother in particular, but in terms of my own development, I don't feel like I suffered because of it. I think that my parents did a fantastic job of helping to raise me to be a strong woman."[2] She still is curious about that missing part of her history, but she believes she has not lost anything by being raised by two dads.

Being raised in an LGBT (lesbian, gay, bisexual, and transgender) family also brought her into a life of activism. Growing up, she often accompanied her fathers during their activist activities fighting for LGBT rights. Today, Steinman-Iacullo is a fashion model and lives in New York City. She continues to advocate for LGBT issues with her fathers, who are now married and have been together over forty-five years.

A New Type of Family

The Steinman-Iacullos were among the first LGBT families in the United States. Just decades ago, there were few LGBT families, and many people considered LGBT lifestyles to be shameful and wrong. When people *came out*—publicly declaring their LGBT status—they were often ostracized by others, including family members. The idea that they should be allowed to marry another LGBT person or have a child was inconceivable to many.

Through adoption, a gay couple is able to enjoy precious moments with their baby girl. In most aspects of daily life, LGBT families are like any other families.

But times have changed. According to the most recent figures available, between 2 million and 3.7 million young people under the age of eighteen have at least one LGBT parent. Of these, 200,000 youth are being raised by a same-sex couple. These numbers come from the Williams Institute at the University of California, Los Angeles, School of Law. The institute conducts research on sexual orientation and gender identity law and public policy. Acceptance of both LGBT individuals and families is growing. According to the Pew Research Center, in 2006 only 51 percent of Americans believed that society should accept homosexuality. By 2016, Pew noted, that number had risen to 63 percent. This change in attitude can be attributed to several factors. One has to do with more people talking openly about their LGBT status. This has led to greater acceptance, particularly when people realize some members of their own friends and family are LGBT. The entertainment media, especially television, have also influenced attitudes with more positive and realistic portrayals of LGBT characters.

Changing Laws

Changes in laws have also eased the way for LGBT families. As a result of a landmark 2015 US Supreme Court decision, *Obergefell v. Hodges,* all states now recognize marriage between same-sex couples. Since then, many same-sex partners have chosen to marry. In 2017, according to a Gallup poll, 10.2 percent of LGBT individuals were married to someone of the same sex, and another 6.6 percent were living with a partner of the same sex but were not married.

Other laws have expanded rights for LGBT parents in custody arrangements stemming from divorce and in foster care and adoption cases. In 2017, for instance, the Supreme Court ruled that the US Constitution requires states to list married same-sex couples on their children's birth certificates. The decision confirmed that the court's decision in *Obergefell* protects all rights relating to marriage, not simply the recognition of marriage. This means that however a same-sex married couple has children, via adoption, surrogacy, or other means, both parents have the same parental rights to the children. For example, if one parent were to die, the other would automatically gain custody as he or she was considered the other lawful parent. These laws protect the status of parents in LGBT families despite whether they are biologically related to their children.

Diversity in LGBT Families

Although LGBT families share that one characteristic, they are as diverse as any other group of families. Some families are multiracial. Some families are headed by a single parent, and others have two parents. Some LGBT families may have children through adoption, and others have biological children.

Multiracial LGBT families are increasing as the result of adoption. One LGBT couple, who started off as foster parents, ended up adopting their foster children, who happened to be different races from their own. This couple blogs about their experiences to help others who are dealing with similar situations. "We are white adoptive parents to 3 siblings adopted transracially through foster care," they write on their blog, *Fostermoms*. "As a mixed-race, queer family of 5, we find ourselves interfacing daily with the challenges that arise when life merges at the intersections of transracial adoption, foster care, LGBT parenting and working for social change."[3]

As with other families, in some LGBT families there is only one parent. A gay man named Terry Snider wanted to be a father and always planned to do so with a partner. However, at age thirty-eight he found himself single and without children. He decided it was time to follow his dream of fatherhood. "Some friends reminded me that I wasn't getting any younger," Snider says. "By then I must admit my thinking was different. I learned how many kids are in foster care that really want families. I thought it made sense to help a child who was already here."[4] Snider became a foster father to three-year-old Vincent and later adopted him.

Allowed to Be a Parent

Forty years ago, openly gay parents were fighting for visitation and custody rights after divorce. At the time, their rights to see their own children were not protected due to their LGBT status. In 1974 a custody case regarding LGBT parental rights was heard by the New Jersey Superior Court. In this case, a man and woman with three children had divorced. The woman, who had primary custody of their children, requested that the court limit visitation rights with the father, who had come out as gay. She asked that he not be able to have his children stay in his home overnight. The judge ruled that a father's sexual orientation is not in itself a reason to deny him child visitation. However, because of the father's political activism on LGBT causes, the judge's order prevented the father from taking his children with him on political marches or having other gay men over while they were visiting. Despite these limitations, this ruling marked the first time a court in the United States had acknowledged the visitation rights of gay fathers.

Vincent is now a typical teen, an honor student, and a black belt in tae kwon do. Being a father, Snider says, has been the most amazing experience of his life.

Like Snider, many LGBT singles and couples have turned to adoption as a path to parenthood. Statistics show that same-sex couples are more likely to be raising adopted children than heterosexual couples. According to the Williams Institute study, 13 percent of LGBT families included an adopted child in 2015. This contrasts with 3 percent of heterosexual couples who have adopted children.

Bryan and Liberty and their three children are another example of an LGBT family. The couple adopted three boys who were siblings with the same biological mother but were living in separate foster homes. Children in foster care often have emotional and other special needs because of the trauma they have experienced. So Bryan and Liberty prepared themselves through

Marital Status of LGBT Americans

Two years after the US Supreme Court ruling that legalized same-sex marriage in all fifty states, marriages of LGBT adults continued to rise. According to a Gallup poll, 10.2 percent of LGBT adults were married to a same-sex spouse in 2017—a continuation of the upward trend that began after the 2015 ruling in *Obergefell v. Hodges*. The poll did not look at the number of LGBT couples with children, but experts note that marriage is often a precursor to having or adopting children—among both LGBT and heterosexual couples.

	Pre-*Obergefell* decision	Year 1 Post-*Obergefell* decision	Year 2 Post-*Obergefell* decision
Married to same-sex spouse	7.9%	9.6%	10.2%
Living with same-sex partner	12.8%	10.1%	6.6%
Single/Never married	47.4%	49.9%	55.7%
Living with oposite-sex partner	4.8%	5.0%	4.2%
Married to opposite-sex spouse	14.2%	13.6%	13.1%
Divorced	7.1%	6.4%	5.4%
Separated	2.5%	2.2%	2.1%
Widowed	2.8%	2.9%	2.2%

Source: Jeffrey M. Jones, "In U.S., 10.2% of LGBT Adults Now Married to Same-Sex Spouse," June 22, 2017, Gallup. http://news.gallup.com.

parenting classes. They encourage other LGBT people to follow the same process to become parents. "For all the ups and downs of parenting, if I step back and look at where our boys' lives were most likely headed just four years ago with no family to call their own, it was a bleak outlook," says Bryan. "Now I look at them thriving, learning, growing, and generally happy kids (except when in trouble or doing homework). It's amazing what a stable loving environment can do for a child. You don't have to be a perfect person to be a parent, you just have to have the ability to love and be loved."[5]

Coming Together in Different Ways

Like other families, LGBT families come together in different ways. Craig, who is both gay and single, always wanted a large family. He adopted three boys—ages three, four, and five—in 1998. Two years later he adopted their older sister, who was ten years old at the time. The following year Craig decided to further expand his family. He became a foster parent to two boys, whom he later adopted. They were nine and ten years old at the time of the adoption.

> **"You don't have to be a perfect person to be a parent, you just have to have the ability to love and be loved."[5]**
>
> —Bryan, an LGBT father

Becoming a parent to children of a different race and helping them deal with the difficult experiences in their early lives has not been easy, Craig says, but the joy of being a parent outweighs the hardships. He explains,

> Many of the kids in foster care come with past baggage. They desperately need love but will push buttons until they are certain that their father(s) really care. Periods of incredible joy may be met with a day of backsliding. On those long days, patience is the guiding force. One slip of a father's tongue will be long remembered and can easily erode the trust that he worked so hard to build.[6]

Some LGBT families come together with the help of reproductive technologies. Lindsey Steinert, who has two dads, recalls the story they told her about how they became a family. Her parents used a surrogate. This involved a woman who was artificially inseminated with sperm from one of Steinert's fathers. The surrogate carried the baby and gave birth to her. Because the birth involved the woman's fertilized egg, she is the biological mother. "My birthmother lived in a different state so the day after

Media Beginnings

Honest portrayals of LGBT families on television have contributed to greater public acceptance. The first television program to depict an LGBT parent was the 1972 television movie *That Certain Summer*, which was shown on NBC. In it, actor Hal Holbrook plays a divorced father who has come out as gay and has started a new life with a male partner. The movie depicts the relationship between the man and his teenaged son, who is grappling with the idea of having a gay father. It was a groundbreaking show, exploring LGBT parenting and portraying an LGBT couple in a sensitive and positive manner. According to Holbrook, who is proud of his role in the movie, "When you can do something decent that touches people's hearts and their minds, so you feel like you actually accomplished something."

Quoted in Revolvy, "That Certain Summer." www.revolvy.com.

I was born my parents boarded a plane to bring me home with them, and mid-flight one of the flight attendants started asking them where my mother was, and why they were traveling with a newborn," Steinert writes. "While they attempted to explain, their efforts weren't successful, and their flight was greeted by the FBI who were responding to a possible kidnapping—reported by the airline."[7] Steinert says that they were able to work out the situation, and they went on to raise her without any incidents as dramatic as this one.

In Ben Somer's case, his moms chose an anonymous sperm donor and one of them became pregnant through in vitro fertilization. "They decided to conceive through a donor, in part, to avoid the complications that a third parent would bring," Somer explains. "Asking a close male friend to donate, like some couples have done, can create unforeseen consequences."[8] To Somer, life with two moms was just normal life.

The Challenges Continue

Although it has become easier for LGBT individuals and couples to form families, they still face a variety of challenges. Some faith-based adoption agencies will not place children with LGBT individuals or couples—and this practice has support in some states. Likewise, people who oppose LGBT rights sometimes forbid their kids from associating with kids from LGBT families.

> **"I know you don't get to pick your parents, but if I could, I wouldn't change a thing."[9]**
>
> —The son of John Groneman, an LGBT father

Despite these challenges, many kids and teens in LGBT families cannot imagine living any other way. John Groneman, a gay man, became a father with a heterosexual woman, who was his friend, because they both wanted children. Despite raising their two children in the same house, they are not a couple and parented only as friends. Growing up in this unique situation, his sons always knew his father's sexual orientation, and they understood that their family setup was unusual. But this did not affect them negatively. When he was a teen, Groneman's youngest son posted this message on his father's Facebook page: "I know you don't get to pick your parents, but if I could, I wouldn't change a thing."[9]

Chapter Two

How I See Myself and My Family

Young people in LGBT families face challenges and issues that youth in more traditional families do not. Understanding their origins, dealing with a nontraditional parenting setup, and even encountering prejudices are part of their lives. As they deal with these issues, many still feel they experience a childhood similar to their friends—going on family vacations, studying for school exams, playing sports, and hanging out with friends. Their experiences, both positive and negative, shape their personalities and how they view life.

Parents Are Parents

Young people who have LGBT parents grow up knowing that their families are a little different from other families. Even knowing this, many feel that they have had as normal a childhood as anyone else. Zach Wahls lived with his family in Wisconsin and Iowa, enjoying a childhood that involved church activities, attaining the Eagle Scout level in Boy Scouts, playing football for his high school, and writing for the school newspaper. Wahls also grew up with two moms, which led to teasing and worse. Despite some unpleasant encounters, he considers himself lucky to have two great parents who were active in his life. By the time he was a teenager, he became politically active, speaking out for LGBT rights to marry and have families. Talking to a group of legislators about what it means to grow up with two moms, Wahls said, "My family eats together, goes to church on Sunday and goes on vacations, just like you. The sense of family comes from the commitment we make to each other. To work through the hard times, so we can enjoy the good ones. It comes from the love that binds us. That's what makes a family."[10]

Like Wahls, Jordan Waller grew up with only moms. Waller initially lived with his biological mother and her female partner. After the couple split up, his mother formed a relationship with another woman, who also helped raise him. While growing up, he knew no other families like his, so he usually kept the details of his family makeup to himself. At home, however, daily life with his moms was filled with much silliness, laughing, and happiness, which shaped how he views his childhood. "My mothers went to a lot of effort to have me, and I grew up in a very happy home," Waller explains. "And no family is perfect. The key thing is to understand that families come in all shapes and sizes, and the important thing is being wanted and being loved, and having your needs met as a child in that family—and mine undoubtedly were."[11]

Taisce Gillespie also grew up with two moms and always felt secure, no matter how others treated them or him. Gillespie's childhood memories include watching television with his moms and brothers, being read books at bedtime, and music nights with friends and family who got together to play music. "I grew up in an environment of abundant love, this makes it impossible to feel like I could possibly have lacked for anything," Gillespie writes. "Love is the key element in a child's development, food and shelter are obviously needed too, but if a child is unconditionally loved it will thrive."[12] As these stories show, many young people who have LGBT parents grew up feeling loved and secure. They also grew up knowing that their families were a little bit different from other families.

Dealing with Differences

Usually, it is early on when children of LGBT parents realize that they are different from other kids. Hannah was in preschool bragging about her two moms when she realized that her family situation was not typical. Although it was not an unpleasant realization, it was a surprising one because she had thought of her family as just like any other. "Other kids would be in the elevator at preschool with their father, and they'd be like 'Why don't I have two mommies like Hannah?'"[13] she recalls.

As they get older, some kids and teens from LGBT families may also learn that their origins are different than other kids. Some learn that their parents used reproductive technologies—such as an anonymous sperm donor—to create a family. Children born this way usually do not learn the identity of the donor. A twenty-six-year-old, who writes anonymously, explains that she was born

A swimming pool and a sunny day provide an opportune moment for family fun. Growing up with two moms might look different from the outside, but to these kids all that matters is that they have two loving, supportive parents.

to an LGBT couple thanks to artificial insemination and an anonymous sperm donor. While she describes her childhood as happy, she has always wondered about the man who was the sperm donor. "My parents told me about the basics of my conception as soon as I was old enough to understand enough to wonder why I didn't have a dad, unlike most of my friends," she writes. "I had a happy normal(ish) childhood. . . . I always knew I was loved and wanted, and I don't think my parents were wrong for deciding to conceive using a donor. . . . However, I always have been, and still am, SO curious about my donor."[14]

Young people who are adopted by LGBT individuals or couples often wrestle with the same feelings and experiences of other adopted children. They might wonder about the birth parents they never knew. Or, if they are older, they might struggle to understand or accept a difficult past. This is in addition to accepting a new family that might not look like the families of other people they know. Zac, who was adopted from foster care, struggled more with the knowledge of his early years than with the fact that his adoptive parents were both men. Zac had lived in twelve different foster homes over a period of three years before he received news that a couple, Arturo and Dave, wanted to adopt him. Zac did not think twice about them being gay—he was happy to find a stable home.

> **"They are my parents and they are always here when I need them."[15]**
>
> —Zac, who was adopted by two dads

Despite that happiness, he had a rough start with his new family. He rebelled and acted out. He stole his parents' credit cards and shoplifted, but even then he saw that his dads stood by him. Years later he wrote them a poem, telling them what they mean to him. "They are my parents and they are always here when I need them," Zac writes. "When it is dark they are the light. When I feel frightened and chills. They are the warmth I feel."[15]

Life Changes

Erin Best Margolin was fifteen when her parents told her they were divorcing. And then her father delivered a bombshell: he told his daughter that he was gay. At first, she felt angry and confused. She felt like she did not know her parents anymore. She felt alone. "Not only are your parents splitting and the family is falling apart, but then also suddenly your dad is gay," she says. She remembers crying and feeling that her whole life was changing and there was nothing she could do to stop it.

The years that followed were challenging, but Margolin eventually accepted the changes in her family. She and her dad have remained close. To assist other young people who feel confused or lost when a parent comes out as LGBT, she helped create the Gay Dad Project. The goal of the website is to provide a place for these young people to share their feelings and experiences—and to feel less alone.

Mitch Weber, "Gay Dad Project Helps Kids Coping with Divorce, Parent's Sexuality," KSHB News, March 5, 2013. www.kshb.com.

Open Communication

Open communication between parents and children can help kids deal with whatever challenges they encounter in life. This communication can be even more important for young people growing up with LGBT parents. It can help them develop a strong self-image even as other people question their origins and family dynamic. Part of this communication involves the parents explaining to their children what it means to be LGBT and how they became a family. "Oh, I've known that for years," twelve-year-old Caleb Foster says when asked how he came into the world. "My uncle gave sperm and Mommy had me."[16] Because he has known this fact for a long time, Caleb has been able to understand and accept that his family is a little different from other families.

Similarly, Mikaela Graham-Radford, twenty-one, and her twin sister, Zoë, understood that their family was untraditional from a young age. They were adopted from Romania. As they grew up, their mothers welcomed questions about LGBT issues and adoption issues, and they encouraged them to write to their biological relatives. When the twins were about eleven, the family traveled to Romania to visit their biological relatives; they still exchange photos and e-mails. Having parents who were so open about their daughters' origins "helped me accept who I am and not be afraid or not be shy,"[17] Mikaela says.

Public or Private

Even young people who love and respect their LGBT parents do not always want to share the details of their family makeup with others. Sometimes they keep this information to themselves to avoid having to face unpleasant questions or responses. This can be kind of lonely. Darius, age thirteen, has two moms whom he loves very much but, he says, he is not forthcoming with others about his parents. This began after elementary school, where he endured unfriendly comments and actions. "People were avoiding me," he says. "I often had lunch alone. I used to find it very stressful."[18] When he started junior high, Darius chose not to tell anyone about his moms. He also decided not to invite friends over to his house, not even his closest friends, to prevent other kids from finding out about his parents.

> **"I often had lunch alone. I used to find it very stressful."[18]**
>
> —Darius, the child of lesbian moms

Heather, a third-grader, has taken a different approach. She is frank with others about the fact that she has two moms, and she even gets frustrated if they do not immediately understand. When asked how she responds to someone questioning her about why she has two moms, she says, "'[I tell them] I just do.' But they think I have a bigger story than that."[19] Heather's three siblings attended the same school; they also chose to be upfront with others and did not have problems with classmates.

The Feeling of Having Missed Out

Some young people from LGBT families feel that they have missed out on something by not having a mom and a dad. Children from single-parent families often experience similar feelings about growing up with just a mom or just a dad. Katy Faust loves her mom and her mom's female partner, and she experienced much happiness growing up. But now, as an adult, she admits to missing a father. Her biological father left when she was in elementary school, after her parents divorced. "I recognized that while my mother was a fantastic mother . . . she can't be a father," Faust says. "Her partner, an incredible woman—both of these women have my heart—cannot be a father either."[20]

Millie Fontana was raised by two mothers; she also experienced a sense of missing out by not having a father in her life. "Growing up, I wanted a father. . . . I felt it within me that I was missing a father before I could even articulate what a father was," Fontana writes. "I knew that I loved both of my parents, but I could not place my finger on what it is I was missing inside myself."[21]

For Faust and Fontana, the feeling of loss impacted their overall view of LGBT parenting. Although they love their parents, as adults they do not agree with their choices to parent. Others, however, in similar situations, also felt the loss of not having a mother or a father in their lives but accepted their situations and focused on the love that they did have.

Character Effects

There is a saying that differences make people stronger. Many people who have LGBT parents say their experiences have done more than that. They say their experiences have helped them develop empathy and other important character traits. Rebecca believes she is a more empathetic person because of her upbringing. Initially, she was raised in a traditional setting with a mom and a dad who were married to each other. At age three, her mother and father divorced, and her mother announced that she was a

To prevent other kids from finding out about his LGBT parents, one young man never invited anyone to his house after school or on weekends. Consequently, he spent a lot of time at home alone.

lesbian. Both parents shared custody of Rebecca, which meant that she enjoyed a relationship with both of them. She also came to know many of her mother's LGBT friends. Rebecca says that the community of people that she grew up with were very accepting, so having an LGBT mom did not result in many issues. She was, however, aware of prejudices her mom and her mom's LGBT friends endured. "I think it's given me a baseline of empathy for people who are outside of the norm or popular understanding.

Getting a Parent's Perspective

Zachary Matheson grew up with two dads. His parents were the first gay male couple to adopt in California. Matheson says he has all of the typical memories of his childhood. But he decided he wanted to know more about what his parents experienced. He wanted to know their thoughts about being gay parents—and the difficulties they faced by being among the first ones.

Matheson had written articles about growing up as the son of two gay men, but this time he decided to interview his father, Tim, and write an article from his dad's perspective. Tim said that although rejection and ignorance were difficult, the hardest part was actually loneliness. "Tim put his career on hold to raise me in a time when men didn't do that," writes Matheson. "Whereas a stay-at-home mom could easily join a network of other supportive moms, Tim was largely on his own. In the first few years, he encountered few stay-at-home dads, and even fewer gay dads. Without that network, he often felt isolated. Alone." As the years went on, it got easier and people became more accepting. Matheson adds that both of his dads say that being his father has been one of the most amazing experiences of their lives.

Zachary Matheson, "The Hardest Part of Being a Gay Parent," *Huffington Post*, June 28, 2016. www.huffingtonpost.com.

It was really good to have that start, and to experience as wholly normal and boring something that other people really fear and hate," Rebecca explains. "It's made me question other things that people fear and hate a lot more."[22]

Sharon Shattuck had a similar, though different, experience that she believes helped her develop compassion for other people. Shattuck has a transgender parent. She is now a filmmaker who has created *From This Day Forward*, a documentary about her family's experiences concerning the transition of her father from male to female while Shattuck was a child. As a child, Shattuck would not admit to others that her father was a female because of the reactions. But as she grew older, she realized she was much more accepting of LGBT people she encountered in college and in the world at large. "Growing up, all I wanted was to be from a 'normal' family," says Shattuck. "But now, I'm grateful that my family is different. It's made me more compassionate toward other people's differences."[23]

"It's made me more compassionate toward other people's differences."[23]

—Sharon Shattuck, whose father is transgender

Anna Thorne believes that growing up with two moms also influenced her in a positive way. She says that the outside influences of society, people's questions, and teasing made her question herself, but her parents helped her figure out who she is. "This is the influence," Thorne writes about her parents—and gay parents, in general. "They create smart, fair-minded people who want to change society for the better, who want to overcome stereotypes and create a safe environment for everyone."[24] Thorne's experience has helped her accept herself and her family and has inspired her to work for equality in the world around her. For Thorne and others who grow up in LGBT families, the challenges they experience, the people they meet, and the way their parents deal with issues have all influenced who they are.

Chapter Three

How the World Sees Me and My Family

At some point in their lives, most young people growing up with LGBT parents have to contend with the attitudes and opinions of people outside their families. Youth in LGBT families face a wide spectrum of reactions—from merely inquisitive at one end to belligerent at the other. These reactions can influence how young people feel about themselves and their families, and they can lead them to react in different ways.

Peer Reaction

Typically, kids experience the first reaction to having LGBT parents when they go to school or first start interacting with other children. Early on, these reactions are usually expressions of curiosity or questioning. Other kids might ask why they have two moms or two dads or where their father or mother is.

As kids get older, the questions sometimes turn into teasing and even bullying. Max Blacker was seven before he experienced any negativity directed at his family. Blacker has grown up with two dads in Los Angeles, which is a city that is generally accepting of LGBT persons. One of his fathers, David Blacker, recalls the first time his son came home upset about a peer's reaction to his family. According to Blacker, Max told him the following about what happened:

> My friend (we'll call him MB, short for misinformed boy) MB said being gay is illegal. Max explained to his friend that his dads were gay and that it's totally normal and most

definitely legal (yes, Max actually uses the phrase "most definitely," it's the cutest thing ever). His friend wasn't buying it and continued to speak with an all-knowing attitude. This really upset Max.[25]

Blacker told his son there would probably always be people who did not approve of their family. What Max needed to know was that it was their problem, not his.

Some young people find it difficult to make friends once classmates learn that they have LGBT parents. Often this is due to the attitudes of their classmates' parents. Early on, Sophie Mei Lan learned to deal with the fact that some children would not be allowed to be her friend. Her father came out as gay when Lan was three, and he and her mother divorced. As she grew up, Lan spent half of her time living with her father and his partner, whom she considers her stepfather. When the parents of her peers learned of her situation, they were not always accepting and warned their children to stay away from her. "As a child growing up, I just accepted that some kids weren't allowed to play at my dad's house. I think their parents were scared they'd catch the 'gay bug' off my dads or me (I might carry it too!),"[26] Lan writes. As she grew older, she felt these reactions made her a stronger person, and she was proud of her family; nonetheless, such reactions were still hurtful.

Bullying

Intrusive questions and being made to feel different can be uncomfortable, but some youth in LGBT families experience worse. They are bullied and harassed. Although schools have zero-tolerance bullying policies, students still find ways to bully. And, as bullies typically look for something different about others to prey upon, a person with an LGBT parent often makes a prime target. The likelihood of bullying and its extent depends on the openness of one's community and how bullying is dealt with by schools and parents.

Negative reactions to one's family can be hurtful, but they can also make a person stronger. One young woman learned not to worry about the comments of outsiders, instead choosing to feel pride in herself and her family.

When David was young, he knew no one besides himself who had two dads. He worried about how other kids would react to his family, so he only let certain kids come over to his house. Once in high school, however, his secret came out. During one of his classes, the teacher put a box at the front of the room and told the students to write down any questions, anonymously, and put them in the box. At the next class, the teacher would answer the questions. David wrote three questions: Is it wrong to have two fathers? How can a baby be born with two fathers? If a boy has two fathers, can he marry a girl? The next time the class met, David anxiously waited to hear her answers. "The teacher took out the pieces of paper and began to answer some of the questions," he writes. "Finally, she got to my piece of paper and read my questions aloud. The classroom erupted with laughter and someone yelled, 'Who's got fags for folks?' Someone else answered: 'I bet you it's David, because he's got two last names, one from each dad!' Laughter filled the air."[27] David raced from the classroom to his house and told his parents about what had happened.

The reaction of his classmates was deeply hurtful. But his fathers sat and talked to him about why his mother had left when he was a child, how his dad and stepfather got together, and what it was like for them as a gay couple. After this conversation, David felt like a weight had been lifted from him; he finally understood more about himself and his family. He eventually changed schools. At his new school, he started out being more open about himself and his family—and, in the process, he discovered there were other students from LGBT families like his.

Dealing with Negativity

Young people from LGBT families have to determine how they will respond to negative reactions from not only their peers but also people in society who do not accept their families. They may experience negative attitudes firsthand from other people but also from viewing the news and social media. Young people react in different way to disapproval of their parents or themselves because they are a part of LGBT families.

Some young people decide to deal with disapproval by trying to avoid it. They might try to keep their family makeup secret. Rather than deal with questions and possible bullying, they keep their parents' LGBT status to themselves. Danielle Silber grew up with gay mothers and encountered discrimination, such as her mothers being referred to with gay slurs, as a child. So when she started middle school, she decided to keep her family makeup a secret. "In middle school, because of pervasive homophobia and taunting, I didn't tell any of my new friends in school about my family to the point where I wouldn't invite them to my birthday parties,"[28] Silber says. Silber did not tell her parents that she hid their status because of her fear of bullying. She did not

> **"In middle school, because of pervasive homophobia and taunting, I didn't tell any of my new friends in school about my family."[28]**
>
> —Danielle Silber, the daughter of two moms

want her parents to know that she was afraid to stand up for her family even though she was proud of them.

Other youth react to mean or biased comments by not allowing them to affect how they feel about themselves. They regard any negative attitudes, whether from people they personally encounter or from people who are speaking in a public setting, as the other person's problem. Kia, thirteen, has grown up with two moms. Her moms split up when she was young, and one formed another partnership with another woman. Kia remembers being more bothered by her moms' breakup and separation than by the fact that she has two moms. Kia has found that most people are not shocked by her situation, but she still prepares herself for different types of reactions. "If you ever tell somebody about your two moms and they say mean stuff, don't let it get to you," Kia says. "If they are your real friends, they won't judge you. At some point everybody is going to know, and it's going to be fine. It won't be a big thing forever. By the next week, there will be new drama at school."[29]

"If you ever tell somebody about your two moms and they say mean stuff, don't let it get to you."[29]

—Kia, the daughter of two moms

Still others feel anger and shock at the attitudes people express toward them and their families. Julia Bleckner, who has two moms, felt confused by laws that she felt unfairly targeted LGBT families. "When I was 10, I learned that my parents had never gotten married, because same-sex marriage was illegal," Bleckner writes. "That didn't compute. I had loving, dedicated parents, yet those in power were denying them the right to be a legal family?"[30] This was in the years just before same-sex marriage became legal and before adoption by LGBT people became acceptable. Because of the laws at the time, one of her moms could not adopt her since she was not legally married to Bleckner's biological mom. To Bleckner, the idea that the government did not recognize her family as a family was alarming and wrong.

A Commercial Breaks New Ground

Honey Maid, the international graham cracker company, produced a commercial in 2016 that broke boundaries and touched hearts. In the commercial, a father comes to terms with the fact that his son is gay, and in a committed relationship, and that the couple has children. The father tells his son that he was at first shocked to learn that his son's partner was a man, but now he feels he has two sons. The commercial continues to show the father, his son, the son's partner, and their children, and it ends with the father saying, "I think any child would be lucky to have two dads like you." The commercial received a negative reception from conservative groups that oppose same-sex marriage and LGBT families. LGBT families and others who support LGBT rights, on the other hand, applauded the company for its sensitive portrayal of changing family dynamics.

Curtis Wong, "Honey Maid's Latest 'Wholesome' Ad Will Melt Your Heart," *Huffington Post*, April 6, 2016. www.huffingtonpost.com.

Since childhood, she has been active in the fight against laws that discriminate against LGBT families.

Religion and Families

Young people from LGBT families often face yet another fight. This one involves religion. Religion is important in the lives of many Americans, including people from LGBT families. Different religions have different views on LGBT individuals, marriage, and parenting. Some are entirely accepting of same-sex marriage and parenting. Others are not. Young people who are being raised in a particular faith can experience real turmoil if their faith does not accept them and their family. In contrast, feelings of acceptance by one's faith can bring real comfort.

Certain faiths and denominations have fully accepted LGBT members. They allow same-sex marriage, baptism, and other important religious rituals to take place in their houses of worship, and they encourage participation by all families who wish to take part in their religious services. For example, the Episcopal Church, a Christian denomination, welcomes LGBT individuals and families and allows LGBT wedding ceremonies within the church. This type of acceptance has allowed youth in LGBT families to feel more comfortable both with their families and their faith and provides them with an accepting community.

Other religions do not accept LGBT marriage or believe that LGBT couples or individuals should have or raise children. The Church of Jesus Christ of Latter-day Saints (aka Mormons) is one of these. In 2015 Mormon officials announced a policy that children living in same-sex households may not be blessed as babies or baptized until they are eighteen. Once they reach eighteen, if they wish to join the church, they must disavow the practice of same-sex partnerships or marriage and stop living within their LGBT household. However, the church later clarified that if a child in a same-sex household was already baptized, his or her status would not be affected. Prior to this ruling, many local Mormon churches embraced a more open attitude toward LGBT members. After the policy announcement, over two thousand LGBT members and others who did not agree with the policy announced they were leaving the church.

Paul Sautter-Walker grew up Mormon, and his faith is a major part of his life. He has lived with the same man for nineteen years, and they married once same-sex marriage became legal. The couple has four children and were raising all of them as Mormons. Three of their children had already been baptized in the church, and their youngest was preparing for his baptism when the policy was announced in 2015. The baptism had to be put on hold. "We thought we'd really like to be able to raise them with some sense of religious understanding or some sense of spiritual knowledge,"[31] said Sauter-Walker. Instead, the family is leaving the church. The Sautter-Walkers do not want their children to be part of a faith that rejects them and their parents.

Entertainment Influences

The entertainment industry also is a strong influence on public perceptions. Its portrayals of LGBT individuals and families have changed over time. Both on television and in movies, stereotypical depictions of the past have given way to more realistic and complex characters and story lines. Television shows and movies can influence public attitudes toward LGBT families, especially when viewers do not interact with or know any LGBT families.

The popular comedy television show *Modern Family* features an LGBT family that consists of two gay dads and their daughter, whom they adopted from Vietnam. The show portrays the family in a loving light. It also takes on common concerns of LGBT families.

In the popular television series *Modern Family* two of the characters (pictured) are a married gay couple who have an adopted daughter. Series like this one portray gay families in a more realistic and loving way than older television shows do.

These include the desire for acceptance by the public and family members as well as encountering bias in laws and public perceptions. Lindsey Steinert says she sees a real difference in attitudes toward families like hers, and she thinks shows like this one have something to do with that change. "In 2017 with shows like 'Modern Family' and 'Orange is the New Black' where same-sex relationships are depicted as 'the norm,' it's becoming increasingly hard to believe—let alone recall—a time when having same-sex parents *wasn't* considered 'trendy' or 'cool,'"[32] Steinert says.

> **"TV has been a powerful influence because it brings the lives of gays and lesbians into people's homes and that has increased people's understanding."[33]**
>
> —Michael Lombardo, the programming president of HBO

Industry experts attribute the public's growing acceptance of LGBT individuals and families partly to the entertainment industry. "TV has been a powerful influence because it brings the lives of gays and lesbians into people's homes and that has increased people's understanding,"[33] says Michael Lombardo of the cable network HBO. HBO has brought the gay-themed plays *Angels in America* and *The Normal Heart* to television and has prominently featured gay characters, some with children, on such series as *Six Feet Under*, *Sex and the City,* and *Looking.*

Turning Negatives into Positives

Although the public perception of LGBT families has become more positive overall, some segments of society still have negative views and misconceptions. Young people in LGBT families are aware of these viewpoints and deal with them daily. Some believe these negative experiences have made them stronger and have also brought their families closer together.

Taisce Gillespie, who was raised by two moms, is one of these people. He has turned negative experiences into positive action,

School Assignments

Young people from LGBT families have come to expect a variety of reactions from peers at school. Reactions from teachers are sometimes harder to deal with. Often, LGBT parents will talk with teachers and school administrators to ensure they are aware of the family's dynamic. The goal is to prevent problems and misunderstandings, but these conversations cannot avoid all uncomfortable situations. For example, school assignments such as family trees or making a Father's Day cards can leave a child or teen feeling upset and misunderstood. "I actually got in a fight with a kindergarten substitute teacher who insisted that I must have a dad, because everyone has a dad," remembers Jamie, who was raised by her lesbian mother. "We were making Father's Day cards, and I was adamant that I did not have a dad. She didn't believe me."

Gabriela Herman, *The Kids*, 2017. https://thekids.gabrielaherman.com.

becoming an advocate for LGBT rights. He also believes that the negativity he and his family endured made his mothers better parents. "I feel that because society has generally forced them at some point to stop and really consider who and what they are, that they often have an added depth or wisdom. This is an invaluable asset to any would-be parent,"[34] Gillespie writes. Gillespie believes that ultimately the wisdom his parents developed, and the unconditional love they provided him, far outweighed any disapproval of others.

Chapter Four

Living in the Public Eye

The debate over LGBT rights is continually in the news these days. This puts young people from LGBT families front and center in that debate. Some see this as a chance to communicate their feelings to the world and thus influence the debate. Others want nothing to do with it, wishing to live their lives like anyone else. But even those who choose not to get actively involved in LGBT political issues are sometimes drawn into the discourse.

Jesse Gilbert has two moms. He has always been aware of the debate over the legitimacy of LGBT families. However, he was never pushed by his family to tell his story or in any way involve himself in debates about LGBT families. Yet he loves his family and could not help but feel an internal pressure to defend it against ignorant comments and personal attacks. When hearing public criticisms of LGBT families or being questioned for his opinions, he felt compelled to respond. "I feel protective of my family," Gilbert explains. "You are aware of the political issue. You are aware of what you are saying and how they will judge you."[35]

The Origins of an Activist

Other young people willingly insert themselves into the debates over LGBT families. Zach Wahls says his experience of growing up in an LGBT family led him on a path to becoming an LGBT rights activist. Wahls was born on July 15, 1991, via artificial insemination. About five years later his mother and her partner held a commitment ceremony to honor their union. They could not marry because same-sex marriage was not legal at the time. Wahls was brought up by both women—his two moms.

Wahls describes his family and childhood as happy and loving. But outside his family he encountered negative reactions. When he was a boy, the family moved to Iowa to live closer to his grandmother. It was there that he first encountered teasing and bullying. His upbringing gave him the strength and wherewithal to deal with the teasing.

It was in eighth grade that Wahls began to realize that other people actually believed that a family like his should not exist. This realization came to him while watching the 2004 Republican convention, an event during which the party's candidate for president was officially chosen. He listened to speakers talking about how they wanted to "protect" marriage by keeping same-sex marriage illegal. "Watching that convention on TV, though, I felt confused, frustrated. Why didn't they think my family was a real family?"[36] Wahls wondered. It was this moment that led to him becoming active in the fight for LGBT rights and, specifically, for the legalization of same-sex marriage.

> **"Why didn't they think my family was a real family?"[36]**
>
> —Zach Wahls, the son of two lesbian mothers

Getting Involved

In high school, Wahls was open about being from an LGBT family. He wrote columns for his high school newspaper about being raised by a lesbian couple. He wanted his classmates to understand that his life was just like their lives except that he had two mothers. While he was still in high school, an Iowa Supreme Court decision legalized same-sex marriage. His own mothers married. In an April 2009 opinion piece in the *Des Moines Register*, Wahls praised the court's decision and explained his view that same-sex marriage should have the same legal status as marriage between a man and a woman.

The issue of same-sex marriage in Iowa did not end with the state Supreme Court ruling, however. While Wahls was

Zach Wahls poses for a photograph with both of his mothers. Wahls chose to become active in the fight for LGBT rights.

in college, conservative organizations assembled campaigns aimed at repealing the law that had legalized same-sex marriage. Wahls stepped up his own political activism, even addressing Iowa's House Judiciary Committee and asking its members not to repeal the law. He spoke about how he was raised by two loving mothers, and what his life was like. Specifically, Wahls explained that his childhood—and his life overall—were not much different from anyone else's childhood or life. He played football in high school, became an Eagle Scout, and was majoring in engineering in college. He also addressed concerns about potential problems from LGBT parenting. "In my 19 years, not once have I ever been confronted by an individual who realized independently that I was raised by a gay couple," said Wahls. "And you know why? Because the sexual orientation of my parents has had zero effect on the content of my character."[37] His testimony was posted on YouTube in 2011; it has been viewed more than 18 million times.

Life Choices

Shortly after this, Wahls withdrew from college to write a book. *My Two Moms: Lessons of Love, Strength, and What Makes a Family* describes the positive impact of growing up with his two mothers. He also continued his political activism as cochair for the Outspoken Generation, the Family Equality Growth Council's national youth advocacy initiative involving the young adult children of LGBT parents. In 2012 Wahls was part of a group of LGBT advocates who lobbied Congress to support legislation that would allow same-sex partners the same hospital visitation rights as married opposite-sex couples. That same year Wahls was asked to speak at the Democratic National Convention. In his speech, he defended marriage equality and same-sex parents.

Wahls eventually returned to college to finish his degree, but he did not sideline his activism. He has continued to advocate for laws that protect LGBT rights. In June 2018 Wahls ran for and won the Democratic primary for Iowa State Senate District 37. The general election was expected to take place in November. His decision to run for office, he says, was influenced by his own experience with not feeling represented by government. He noted that he has fought for his own family and hopes to do the same for others.

Taking a Different Stance

Like Wahls, Katy Faust became an activist after being raised by her lesbian mom and her mother's partner. Yet unlike Wahls, she advocates against same-sex marriage. Faust says that she enjoyed a relatively happy and normal childhood and that she loves her mom and her mom's partner. However, she believes that children are better served by having a mother and a father. Because same-sex marriage deprives them of one or the other, she believes it should not be legal.

Faust's parents divorced when she was young, and her father left shortly after that. Not long after that her mother came out as a lesbian. She and her new partner raised Faust. Often, Faust recalls, she felt pressure to defend her mother's life choices, and she would do so, even though she inwardly did not agree. Although she and her father maintained a relationship, Faust says that she deeply missed having a father actively in her life. This gap is what led her to eventually oppose same-sex marriage. She believes that children do best when they have both a father and a mother. "My parents' divorce has been the most traumatic event in my thirty-eight years of life. While I did love my mother's partner and friends. I would have traded every one of them to have my mom and my dad loving me under the same roof,"[38] Faust writes. On the basis of her experiences, Faust has come to believe that same-sex couples should not raise children because this arrangement deprives them of a mother and a father. Allowing same-sex marriage, she argues, just results in more same-sex couples choosing to have children.

Acting on Her Beliefs

Faust's experiences led her to become an activist in the campaign to oppose the legalization of same-sex marriage. After graduating from college, she founded Them Before Us, an organization dedicated to advancing social policies that encourage

Changing the Boy Scouts

In addition to advocating for LGBT marriage as a result of his life with his two moms, Zach Wahls has also taken on other LGBT issues. One of these issues involved the Boy Scouts of America's ban on gay members and leaders. Wahls spent years in the Boy Scouts and even attained Eagle Scout level. He loved the experiences he had as a Boy Scout, and he wanted to ensure similar opportunities for other boys. In April 2012 Jennifer Tyrrell, a lesbian den mother from Ohio, was ousted from her son's Cub Scout pack. Following this, Wahls founded the Scouts for Equality, a national campaign to end discrimination in the Boy Scouts of America.

Scouts for Equality worked to make people aware of Boy Scout policies against gay people and urged the group's leaders to end the ban. In 2013 the leadership voted to end the ban on gay youth. Wahls's organization continued to pressure the Boy Scouts to also end the ban for adults and allow openly gay adults to be leaders. In 2015 the executive board of the Boy Scouts voted to end the blanket ban on gay adults, achieving the primary goal of Scouts for Equality. The organization continues to work with the Boy Scouts to strengthen policies on diversity and inclusion.

adults to actively respect the rights of children. Faust believes that children have a right to be raised by a father and a mother. In 2012 she began to blog about what she believes are the needs of children and how family structure must support those needs. Her articles about why she does not support same-sex marriage have appeared in *USA Today* and the conservative publication the *Federalist*.

When the US Supreme Court was considering the legality of same-sex marriage in 2015, Faust filed with the court two papers that argued against same-sex marriage. She also wrote a letter to Supreme Court justice Anthony Kennedy expressing her view that "redefining marriage redefines parenthood. Though that might sound fine if you are beyond the age of consent, most children will tell you that if they could order their own world, it would

Opponents of same-sex marriage hold signs proclaiming that children need both a mother and a father. This is also the view of Katy Faust, who was raised by a lesbian mother. Although she loves her mother she does not support LGBT parenting.

be one in which they are being loved and raised by their mother and father."[39] Faust's experience of growing up in an LGBT family impacted the course of her life, and she now works to ensure that children are raised with a mother and a father whenever possible.

Stories of Real Life

Like Wahls and Faust, Lindsey Steinert was raised by LGBT parents and had a desire to communicate her experiences to other people. But unlike Wahls and Faust, she had no desire to become politically active. Instead, she chose the theater as the way to show others what life with two dads has been like. Steinert wrote *Upstream Swimming,* a piece that she also performs. It is a lighthearted look at her life. It includes humorous stories, such as not being able to fill out her mother's maiden name on forms, and deals with the questions that people constantly asked her while she was growing up (such as where her mom was).

> **"Most children will tell you that if they could order their own world, it would be one in which they are being loved and raised by their mother and father."[39]**
>
> —Katy Faust, the daughter of a lesbian mom

Steinert has good memories of her childhood. Early on she understood that her family was not typical, but she does not feel this had any sort of negative influence on her or her siblings. "Five kids, two birthmothers and four beagles later, my parents not only created a loving family, but raised five children who collectively have no interest, despite having the option and ability, to meet their birthmothers," Steinert says. "A phenomenon I can only attribute to my Dad and Pop's parenting, and their insistence that we be surrounded by strong, female figures."[40]

Steinert went on to college and graduated with a degree in acting. After graduation, Steinert realized she had something important to say and decided theater was the best place to say it. She wanted to show people with more traditional families what her family was like. She wanted them to understand that there really was not much difference between them. "When I graduated college in 2014 and realized that people were *still* shocked to learn that I have two gay dads, I knew it was important for me to use my unique position as a child of same-sex parents to contribute to the 'normalization' of families like mine,"[41] she writes. She first performed her one-woman show in October 2014 in New York City. She has since performed it in a variety of locations and festivals.

> **"I knew it was important for me to use my unique position as a child of same-sex parents to contribute to the 'normalization' of families like mine."[41]**
>
> —Lindsey Steinert, the daughter of two gay dads

Steinert believes that her words are making a difference. "I feel it's my responsibility to insure such progress continues," she writes. "And the best way I know how to do that is by sharing my story with others, and encouraging potential same-sex parents that the only way to alter society's understanding of what it means to be a 'normal' family, is to redefine it."[42]

A Traumatizing Childhood

Denise Shick has also experienced life with an LGBT parent, but for her the experience was not a happy one. When Shick was nine, her father told her that he felt he was meant to be a woman. Rather than be called Harold, his given name, he began the transition to becoming Becky. He dressed in women's clothes and used hormones to help his body develop more feminine traits. Shick writes that he sometimes borrowed her clothes and make-up, and she often felt he was jealous of her femininity. She longed for a father who would support her, but instead she felt that he gave her no support and seemed to resent her for being female. Now that her father is dead, she says she misses him, but the person she misses is Harold, not Becky. Shick writes, "I miss all those times when he accepted the reality that he was Harold, a man—a husband, father, and grandfather. I don't miss Becky, or those transition times when my father gave in to his transgender impulses."[43]

Shick founded and is the executive director of Help 4 Families. It is a Christian ministry that tries to help family members with a loved one who, in the organization's words, is "gender confused."[44] She has also written articles and books about her experience of growing up with a transgender father and her belief that transgender people are acting on unnatural impulses. These impulses, she believes, are harmful to families.

On the basis of her view that every child deserves a mother and a father, and that life with LGBT parents is confusing and stressful for children, she also has written articles opposing LGBT

Marching for Their Dad

When Kelle was eight years old, her father came out as gay. After her mother and father divorced, she spent her weekends with her father. Although it took adjustment, she accepted her father's new life and supported him. Meanwhile, Kelle's mother joined a church that taught that homosexuality was a sin, and she grew up seeing what she considered unjust treatment of her father by this church and other groups. As adults, both Kelle and her sister have taken part in marches in support of LGBT rights and have advocated for gay rights. Kelle's father does not march, as he says he is not a marching type, but supports his children's doing so. "We march in the gay parades while my dad chooses to watch us march for him," Kelle explains. "He applauds our marching even though he doesn't like to do the parade thing himself. His gay advocacy is subtle; ours is loud. In all forms of advocacy, I'm realizing both are important."

Kelle Hampton, "An Interview with My Dad on Gay Pride: 'I Am Proud to Be a Child of God. This Is the Gay That the Lord Hath Made," *Kelle Hampton & Enjoying the Small Things* (blog), June 2017. http://kellehampton.com.

parenting and adoption. "I can testify to the emotional strain and confusion that my father's life played in my sexual and gender identity," writes Shick. "I sought out our neighbors for a foster father. Many times I pretended that one of my uncles or a friend's father was my make-believe father. I was so hungry for my father; a transgender 'mom' would not fit that need no matter how badly the adult wished it to."[45]

Voices Being Heard

Being raised in LGBT households gave Shick, Steinert, Wahls, and Faust unique perspectives on a subject that is frequently debated in the public sphere. Though their experiences are their own, all four felt compelled to share, in some way, the details of their lives so that others might understand their point of view.

Chapter Five

Other People Who Have Families Like Mine

The idea of a family headed by an LGBT parent or parents was once fairly shocking. This family dynamic would very likely have been kept secret from just about everyone—including, sometimes, other family members. Few would have been willing to tell their stories publicly—or even privately. But things have changed in recent years. LGBT couples are now free to legally marry. And many are adopting children or taking advantage of reproductive technologies to have their own children. Among those who have publicly talked about their lives in an LGBT family are four well-known individuals: singer and actress Mandy Moore, comedian Kaitlin Colombo, professional basketball player Kenneth Faried, and actor Neil Patrick Harris. Taken together, their stories present a picture of families being families—nothing more and nothing less.

Learning Authenticity

Singer Mandy Moore first came to fame in 1999 with her debut single "Candy." During the next decade, her success as a musician continued; by 2012, Moore was ranked among the top one hundred women musicians by cable and satellite network VH1. In addition to music, Moore has pursued acting. She costarred in the 2001 movie *The Princess Diaries* and starred in the 2002 movie *A Walk to Remember*. She has appeared in several other movies, including as the voice of Rapunzel in *Tangled* (2010). Since 2016, Moore has starred in the television comedy-drama *This Is Us*. Part of what led to success at such an early age, Moore says, was the support of her family.

Moore was born in 1984 to Stacy and Donald Moore in Nashua, New Hampshire. She was the middle child of three kids, including an older brother, Scott, and a younger brother, Kyle. All through Moore's growing-up years, her family was fairly traditional. However, when Moore was twenty-three her mother came out as a lesbian. Moore's mother left her father for another woman. Moore has said that her parents did a great job raising their family, but she thinks it is better that her mother is being true to herself. After her mother came out, both of Moore's brothers came out as gay too. "Everyone's so much happier (now), richer and more fulfilled, being their authentic selves,"[46] Moore says.

Being part of this family has inspired Moore to focus on what is most important in her life, which she believes is finding people you love and being with them. Having an LGBT family has taught her that putting restraints on love because of one's gender is unhealthy. "Nobody is hiding who they are. There are no secrets in our lives," Moore says. "I love and support my mom and my brothers with my whole heart. And nothing makes me happier than seeing anybody live their authentic self, and to choose love. If anyone can find love, I support it, I salute you and I celebrate that."[47]

"I love and support my mom and my brothers with my whole heart."[47]

—Mandy Moore, an actress with gay brothers and a lesbian mother

As part of an LGBT family, Moore has become more aware of LGBT discrimination and is protective of her family members. Although she sees more tolerance in the world than in the past, she also is aware of the negativity that is out there too. This has led her to take a stand against prejudice toward LGBT people. Referring to intolerance toward anyone, she says, "I feel a certain amount of protectiveness. I definitely won't stand for that. But I feel like we're at a time in our culture when we're able to have a much more open dialogue."[48]

Singer and actress Mandy Moore is protective of her lesbian mother and gay brothers. She has spoken out against intolerance toward LGBT individuals.

Early Activism and Career

Like Moore, Kaitlin Colombo started her career in entertainment while still in her teens, and, like Moore, Colombo is from an LGBT family. Colombo is a comedian, actress, and writer. She has appeared on the NBC series *Last Comic Standing* and on the MTV series *The Reality Show*. She continues to appear on television and plays, such as *Showgirls* and *Planet of the Gays*.

Colombo knew from an early age that she wanted to be a comedian, but it was not until she moved with her dad to Los Angeles that the idea really came together. Concerned that she was not meeting people, her dad enrolled her in a teen improv group that did stand-up comedy. She recalls, "Secretly, all I wanted in the world was to write and perform—and stand up, I realized in that moment, was the perfect synthesis of the two."[49] Colombo's talent was noticed while performing with the group. In 1999, at the age of thirteen, she appeared onstage at the Hollywood Improv, a well-known comedy club in Hollywood. Budd Friedman, the owner of the club, came up to her after her set and told her she was funny and to come back. Colombo continued performing. She also wrote a screenplay at age fourteen and sold a television pilot to Fox at age seventeen.

Colombo's material, both in her own writing and her performances, includes a lot of stories about living with a gay father. Her parents had separated when she was young, and her father had been given primary custody. Growing up with an openly gay father brought some challenges. She remembers being able to handle negative comments from other kids easily, but it was comments from adults that hurt her. "I remember talking to my mother's boyfriend, and he asked me, 'What are you going to do when your father dies of AIDS.' Who the hell says that to an eight year old?"[50] said Colombo. At the time, AIDS was considered a fatal disease that mainly afflicted gay men, although medical researchers later learned that any type of sexual encounter—heterosexual or homosexual—can spread the virus that causes AIDS.

Colombo found that her experiences as the child of an LGBT parent fit nicely into her comedy and gave her an outlet for advocating for LGBT rights. She included humorous stories about how her father would make her elaborate costumes, as opposed to buying a Halloween costume, and constantly sing show tunes when she was growing up. When she was seventeen, she wrote a sitcom pilot titled *The Voices Inside My Head*. It was based on her observations of pop culture and its impact on girls as well as her experiences of being raised by a gay father. She performed as a featured stand-up performer on Rosie O'Donnell's R Family Vacations cruise lines, which were cruises for LGBT families, and she has headlined across the country at gay pride events.

Most recently, Colombo has written and performed in plays and musical shows and has written articles and stories, often to advocate for LGBT causes. She founded the Colombo Company, a nonprofit entertainment company dedicated to creating discourse through storytelling, with a specific focus on LGBT and women's issues.

Acceptance

National Basketball Association (NBA) player Kenneth Faried also grew up in an LGBT family. In school, he excelled in sports. After playing center for Morehead State University in Kentucky, in 2011 he was drafted by the Denver Nuggets, and he has been with the team since that time.

Faried was born to Kenneth Lewis and Waudda Faried, and he grew up in Newark, New Jersey. His parents were not married, but they remained together for a short period after Faried's birth. Although he lived with his mother, both parents were active in his life and introduced him to basketball at an early age. His mother had been a star player in high school, and she wanted her son to love the sport.

When Faried was nine, he asked his mother why she and his father were no longer together. That is when she explained that she had realized she was a lesbian. The revelation that his mother was attracted to other women led Faried to question who he was; he wondered if he should be gay because his mother was. He recalls asking her, "'Ma, if you like women, am I supposed to like men? Because you're my role model.' And she said, 'No, no,' and she laughed, and she was, 'Whatever you're happy with. You can like women, you can like men, whatever you're happy with, you're

Coming Out with a Song

Rapper Jay-Z did not grow up knowing his mother was a lesbian. She came out to him when he was an adult. For years, she hid her sexuality from him and his siblings, not wanting to embarrass them. She finally decided to let him know when she met a woman she loved, and she wanted to be open about their relationship. The day she came out to him, he cried, happy that she had found someone to love and that she was able to be true to herself. The same day she told him, Jay-Z responded by writing a song, "Smile," that he and his mom performed together on his 2017 album, *4:44*. On it, Jay-Z raps about how his mother had to pretend to be someone she was not throughout his childhood because she feared how society would view her and her children if she admitted that she was a lesbian.

CBS News, "Jay-Z Says He Cried with Joy When His Mom Came Out to Him as a Lesbian," April 2, 2018. www .cbsnews.com.

perfectly fine.'"[51] Faried also talked to his dad, who explained that just because his mom was a lesbian did not mean that Faried was gay too, but it was okay if he was. As Faried grew older, he realized he was attracted to girls, and he no longer worried about whether he should be gay or not. His experience with learning who he was led him to be more accepting of other people.

When he was about eleven, Faried's mother introduced him to her girlfriend, Manasin Copeland. He immediately liked her and was happy she was a part of his mother's and his life. He wanted someone to be there for his mother, who was battling the disease lupus. Faried began to think of Copeland as his second mother. When the two women decided to marry, Faried's reaction was one of happiness. "When they got married, that showed me what commitment is all about, that there are people out there that can commit, even though for them it really has been the worst of times,"[52] Faried says, speaking of the fact they married despite his mother's challenging medical condition.

NBA basketball player Kenneth Faried says he was teased and insulted as a child because he had two mothers. That experience made him tougher and more resilient, and willing to work for LGBT causes.

Faried says that growing up in an LGBT family also made him tougher. Kids often teased and insulted him. He followed the advice of his father: try to ignore the rude comments, and remember that everyone comes from different types of families. He also knew that he had the support of all three of his parents.

Professional and Private Life Entwined

During his last year in high school, Faried was recruited by Morehead. The university wanted him to play on its basketball team. Although he was nervous about going so far away from his family, Copeland assured him that she would take care of his mother, so he accepted. Eventually his mother underwent a kidney transplant, and her health improved.

During college he excelled at basketball, breaking the National Collegiate Athletic Association Division I rebounding record. With help from dedicated teachers, he was able to pass his courses. In 2011 Faried was drafted by the Denver Nuggets. He decided he wanted to use his newfound status to promote LGBT causes. With his mothers, he attended New York City's Gay Pride Parade in 2012. That same year he also became the first NBA player to work with Athlete's Ally, a group trying to prevent homophobia in sports. After the US Supreme Court ruled that gay marriage was legal in 2015, Faried tweeted, "Love conquers all! #SameSexMarriage finally legal in all 50 States! I'm so happy for the #LGBTCommunity!"[53]

> **"Love conquers all! #SameSexMarriage finally legal in all 50 States! I'm so happy for the #LGBTCommunity!"[53]**
>
> —Kenneth Faried, an NBA player with a lesbian mother

A Parent's Perspective

Although actor Neil Patrick Harris did not grow up as a child in an LGBT household, he understands what it is like to be part of an LGBT family. When he was in his teens, Harris realized he was gay. Today he and his husband have two children, and they both relish the experiences of being a parent.

Harris, who was born in 1973, has been in the spotlight since he was a teen. He starred in the 1990s television comedy *Doogie Howser, MD.* Since then, he has continued to act and sing, taking on a wide range of roles in movies and on television and the stage. He starred in the long-running television sitcom, *How I Met Your Mother* and more recently, starred as Count Olaf in *A Series of Unfortunate Events* on Netflix. He has also hosted the Emmy Awards, the Academy Awards, and the Tony Awards.

After realizing he was gay, Harris came out to his friends and family, but it was not until 2006 that he spoke publicly about being gay. At that point, he realized that he did not want to hide who he was or that he had a boyfriend. And he has been happy with that decision ever since. "I am happy to dispel any rumors or misconceptions and am quite proud to say that I am a very content gay man living my life to the fullest and feel most fortunate to be working with wonderful people in the business I love,"[54] Harris told *People* magazine in 2006.

Married with Kids

Harris started dating David Burtka in 2003. After several years together, they knew they wanted to be parents. "We really, really wanted kids. We really had thought it through financially, emotionally, relationship-wise," says Harris. "We didn't just accidentally get pregnant and decide that now we need to make this work. These kids come into our world with nothing but love."[55]

"We really, really wanted kids. We really had thought it through financially, emotionally, relationship-wise."[55]

—Neil Patrick Harris, a gay actor who is married with two children

Burtka and Harris decided on surrogacy as their route to children. In 2010 they became parents to twins Harper and Gideon. The following year they became engaged after New York legalized gay marriage; in 2014 the couple married in Italy. Harris says they plan to talk with their children about surrogacy (what it means and what it means to them as parents) once their children get a little older. But for now, Harris is focused on just being a good dad, doing many of the same things that other dads do with their kids. "They are your children, Gideon and Harper," he writes in his autobiography, *Choose Your Own Autobiography*. "The ones you worked so hard to get, the ones you waited for so long, and you love them madly, crazily, bottomlessly. When you're home you spend as much time with them as you can."[56]

Vacations for LGBT Families

Actress and comedian Rosie O'Donnell came out as a lesbian in 2002. Prior to that, O'Donnell had adopted her first child, Parker Jaren O'Donnell, as an infant in 1995. She went on to have four children with Kelli Carpenter, who was her partner and then spouse. O'Donnell believed there was a need for LGBT families to relax and enjoy time with other LGBT families, so in 2003 she and Carpenter partnered with travel entrepreneur Gregg Kaminsky to launch R Family Vacations. R Family Vacations caters to LGBT families. On July 11, 2004, its first cruise embarked with sixteen hundred passengers, including six hundred children. On the cruise, there was traditional entertainment and recreational activities in addition to talks about gay parenting issues. Although O'Donnell has since parted with the company, it continues to provide LGBT vacations around the world.

For All to See

The family stories shared by Moore, Colombo, Faried, and Harris are much like any family's stories. And that is the point. Although they are configured a little differently from traditional families, their lives are very much the same as anyone else's.

Source Notes

Chapter One: How American Families Are Changing

1. Quoted in PFLAG New York City, "Staten Island PFLAGers Receive 'One Island, One Pride' Award," 2011. www.pflagnyc.org.
2. Quoted in Emily Anne Epstein, "The Children of Gay Parents Speak for Themselves," *Atlantic*, March 2016. www.theatlantic.com.
3. *Fostermoms* (blog), "About Us," 2018. www.fostermoms.com.
4. Quoted in James Nichols, "One Man's Beautiful Journey to Fatherhood," *Huffington Post*, February 26, 2016. www.huffingtonpost.com.
5. Quoted in Gays with Kids, "Faces of Gay Foster Care Dads and Kids," November 22, 2016. www.gayswithkids.com.
6. Quoted in Gays with Kids, "Faces of Gay Foster Care Dads and Kids."
7. Lindsey Steinert, "A One Woman Show About a Totally Normal Girl," Gays with Kids, 2017. www.gayswithkids.com.
8. Ben Somer, "Meeting My Sperm-Donor Dad," Good Men Project, February 7, 2011. https://goodmenproject.com.
9. Quoted in Gays with Kids, "A Text from a Gay Man's Son Brought Him to Tears," September 10, 2017. www.gayswithkids.com.

Chapter Two: How I See Myself and My Family

10. Quoted in Susan James, "Son of Iowa Lesbians Fights Gay Marriage Ban," ABC News, February 3, 2011. http://abcnews.go.com.
11. Quoted in Joanna Moorhead, "Jordan Waller—'I Told Friends I Had Two Moms,'" *Guardian* (Manchester, UK), December 23, 2017. www.theguardian.com.

12. Taisce Gillespie, “My Wonderful Gay Family: I Was Raised by Two Loving, Beautiful Lesbian Mums,” TheJournal.ie, May 17, 2015. www.thejournal.ie.
13. Quoted in Gabriela Herman, *The Kids: The Children of LGBTQ Parents in the USA*. New York: New Press, 2017, p. 18.
14. Quoted in Anonymous Us, “Who Are You?,” February 17, 2018. https://anonymousus.org.
15. Quoted in Patrick Wallace, “Adopted by Two Gay Dads After a Tumultuous Upbringing, 15-Year-Old Zac Shares a Letter of Love,” *Huffington Post*, February 2, 2016. www.huffingtonpost.com.
16. Quoted in Denise Balkissoon, “The 7 Habits of Highly Effective Lesbian Families,” *Globe and Mail* (Toronto), March 29, 2018. www.theglobeandmail.com.
17. Quoted in Balkissoon, “The 7 Habits of Highly Effective Lesbian Families.”
18. Quoted in Balkissoon, “The 7 Habits of Highly Effective Lesbian Families.”
19. Quoted in Balkissoon, “The 7 Habits of Highly Effective Lesbian Families.”
20. Quoted in Activist Mommy, “Woman Raised by Same Sex Couple Says Children Deserve Both Mother and Father,” September 22, 2017. https://activistmommy.com.
21. Millie Fontana, “Millie Fontana,” Them Before Us, April 11, 2017. https://thembeforeus.com.
22. Quoted in Jia Tolentino, “Interview with a Person Whose Mom Came Out of the Closet,” Hairpin, June 2013. www.thehairpin.com.
23. Quotod in Diana Pearl, “What It’s Really Like to Have a Transgender Parent,” *People*, January 12, 2015. http://people.com.
24. Anna Thorne, “What People Need to Know About Growing Up with Two Moms,” HelloGiggles, September 29, 2014. https://hellogiggles.com.

Chapter Three: How the World Sees Me and My Family

25. Quoted in Gays with Kids, “When a Kid with Two Dads Is Made to Feel Different.” www.gayswithkids.com.

26. Sophie Mei Lan, "10 Things You'll Only Know If You've Grown Up with Gay Parents," Metro, October 14, 2017. http://metro.co.uk.
27. David, "I've Got Two Dads," ReachOut, 2018. https://au.reachout.com.
28. Quoted in Sean Piccoli, "Gay Marriage: 5 Quotes from Children About Family Life with Same-Sex Parents," Newsmax, July 7, 2015. www.newsmax.com.
29. Quoted in Te-Erika Patterson, "My Two Moms," Daily Parent, 2018. http://dailyparent.com.
30. Julia Bleckner, "Don't Use Religion to Cloak Bias Toward LGBT Families," *Los Angeles Times*, September 10, 2014. www.latimes.com.
31. Quoted in Lorena O'Neil, "Rejected Gay Mormon Dads Face Painful Decision About Baptism Policy," *Huffington Post,* December 3, 2015. www.huffingtonpost.com.
32. Steinert, "A One Woman Show About a Totally Normal Girl."
33. Quoted in Scott Collins and Meredith Blake, "Years Before Court Ruling, Pop Culture Shaped Same-Sex Marriage Debate," *Los Angeles Times,* June 28, 2015. www.latimes.com.
34. Gillespie, "My Wonderful Gay Family."

Chapter Four: Living in the Public Eye

35. Quoted in Abigail Garner, *Families Like Mine: Children of Gay Parents Tell It Like It Is.* New York: HarperPerennial, 2005.
36. Quoted in Ryan Grim, "Zach Wahls Speech Backs President Who Backs Gay Marriage," *Huffington Post,* September 9, 2012. www.huffingtonpost.com.
37. Quoted in Susan Donaldson James, "Son of Lesbians Fights Gay Marriage Ban," ABC, February 3, 2011. http://abcnews.go.com.
38. Katy Faust, "Dear Justice Kennedy: An Open Letter from the Child of a Loving Gay Parent," *Public Discourse,* February 2, 2015. www.thepublicdiscourse.com.
39. Katy Faust, "Children Like Me Need a Voice in the Gay Marriage Debate," *USA Today*, April 15, 2014. www.usatoday.com.
40. Lindsey Steinert, "I Had Two Gay Dads Before It Was 'Cool,'" *Huffington Post,* February 9, 2017. www.huffingtonpost.com.
41. Steinert, "I Had Two Gay Dads Before It Was 'Cool.'"
42. Steinert, "I Had Two Gay Dads Before It Was 'Cool.'"

43. Denise Shick, "My Dad Was Transgender. Why I Still Think Gender Cannot Be Changed," Daily Signal, May 25, 2016. www.dailysignal.com.
44. Quoted in Help 4 Families, "Gender Identity," 2017. www.help4families.com.
45. Denise Shick, "I Had a Transgender Parent. Unlike Obama, I Don't Think Transgender Parents Should Be Able to Adopt," Daily Signal, May 26, 2015. www.dailysignal.com.

Chapter Five: Other People Who Have Families Like Mine

46. Quoted in Rachel Desantis, "Mandy Moore's Family Dynamic Is Far from Traditional—Just Like Her 'This Is Us' Kin," *New York Daily News,* October 26, 2017. www.nydailynews.com.
47. Quoted in Aili Nahas, "Mandy Moore Says Her Family Is 'Extraordinarily Close' After Her Mom Left Her Dad for a Woman, 2 Brothers Came Out," *People*, October 26, 2017. http://people.com.
48. Quoted in Nahas, "Mandy Moore Says Her Family Is 'Extraordinarily Close' After Her Mom Left Her Dad for a Woman, 2 Brothers Came Out."
49. Kaitlin Colombo, "BWW Blog Kaitlin Colombo—My First Time," *BroadwayWorld* (blog), February 2, 2001. www.broadwayworld.com.
50. Quoted in Winnie McCroy, "Comedian Kaitlin Colombo Crowdsources for 'GLITORIS' Burlesque," Edge Media Network, February 20, 2015. https://phoenix.edgemedianetwork.com.
51. Quoted in Tom Friend, "Faried Makes His Moms Proud," ESPN, May 14, 2013. www.espn.com.
52. Quoted in Friend, "Faried Makes His Moms Proud."
53. Quoted in Joe Nguyen, "Kenneth Faried, Nuggets Forward, Reacts to Gay Marriage Ruling," *Nuggets Ink* (blog), *Denver Post*, June 26, 2015. http://blogs.denverpost.com.
54. Quoted in *People*, "Neil Patrick Harris, I am a Very Content Gay Man," November 20, 2006. http://people.com.
55. Quoted in Abbie Goldberg, "Life as a Gay Father, Neil Patrick Harris Opens Up to Oprah," *From the Square* (blog), June 7, 2012. www.fromthesquare.org.
56. Neil Patrick Harris, *Choose Your Own Autobiography.* New York: Crown Archetype, 2014. http://nphbook.com.

For Further Research

Books

Carlos Ball, *The Right to Be Parents: LGBT Families and the Transformation of Parenthood*. New York: New York University Press, 2014.

Amanda Baumie, *Legalizing LGBT Families: How the Law Shapes Parenthood*. New York: New York University Press, 2017.

Neil Patrick Harris, *Choose Your Own Autobiography*. New York: Crowne Archetype, 2014.

Gabriela Hermin, *The Kids: The Children of LGBTQ Parents in the USA*. New York: New Press, 2017.

Nancy Mezey, *LGBT Families*. Los Angeles: Sage, 2014.

H.W. Poole, *LGBT Families: Lesbian, Gay, Bisexual, and Transgender*. Broomall, PA: Mason Crest, 2016.

Internet Sources

Emily Epstein, "The Children of Gay Parents Speak for Themselves," *Atlantic,* March 2016. www.theatlantic.com/photo/2016/03/the-kids/472338.

Jessie Moonie, "These States May Make It More Difficult for LGBT Couples to Adopt," *Brides*, April 24, 2018. www.brides.com/story/these-states-may-make-it-more-difficult-for-lgbt-couples-to-adopt.

James Nichols, "These Moms Share Their Incredible Journey to Creating Their Beautiful Family," *Huffington Post,* September 23, 2016. www.huffingtonpost.com/entry/let-love-define-family-sept-22_us_57e411f7e4b08d73b830087d.

Joanne Spataro, "Adventures in Transgender Fertility," *New York Times,* April 24, 2018. www.nytimes.com/2018/04/24/opinion/transgender-fertility-preservation.html.

Lindsey Steinert, "I Had Two Dads Decades Before It Was 'Cool,'" *Huffington Post,* February 6, 2017. www.huffingtonpost.com/entry/i-had-two-gay-dads-decades-before-it-was-cool_us_5899350ae4b061551b3e02e2.

Websites

Hound Mamas (https://houndmamas.wordpress.com). This is a blog written by a woman about her life with her wife and their two children. It includes posts about parenting, discrimination, and other aspects of their lives.

The Next Family (http://thenextfamily.com). This website is for families of all types and provides personal accounts of both children and parents in the families. The website also provides articles on current LGBT family issues and news in addition to articles and books on surrogacy, LGBT families, and adoption.

Proud Parenting (www.proudparenting.com). Proud Parenting provides articles with personal stories of LGBT parenting, news on LGBT legal issues, and information about entertainment featuring LGBT families. Additionally, the website contains pictures and posts by LGBT families.

Index

Picture Credits

Cover: Masarik/Shutterstock.com

6: Africa Studio/Shutterstock.com

10: Maury Aaseng

16: Juanmonino/iStockophoto.com

21: Neeila/Shutterstock.com

26: Monkey Business Images/Shutterstock.com

31: Photofest Images

36: HRC/WENN/Newscom

40: Associated Press

46: Kathy Hutchins/Shutterstock.com

50: Marcos Mesa Sam Wordley/Shutterstock.com

About the Author

Leanne Currie-McGhee lives in Norfolk, Virginia, with her husband, Keith, and daughters, Grace and Hope. She has enjoyed writing educational books for over fifteen years.